I0753755

the village is quiet

PATRICK HARTIGAN

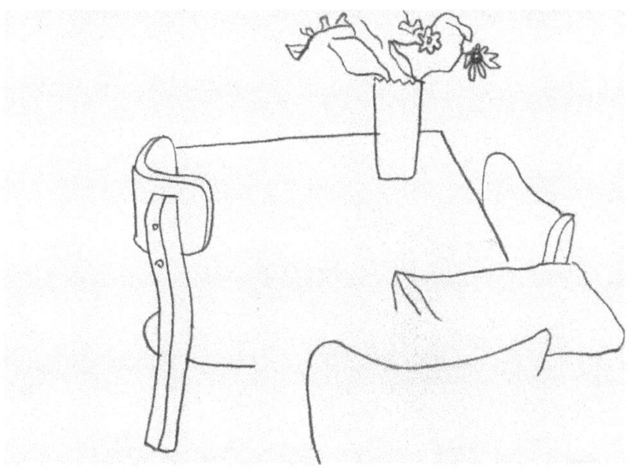

GAZEBO BOOKS – SUMMER HILL – 2021

Goats

Grandpa's goat is ready for mating. It's getting late and there's a heavy mist rolling in when grandma and I take Clementine to the goatherd's house a couple of doors down. In the man's yard there's shit and mud, and some long sticks to control the goats. Grandma is chanting, 'nah nah nah nah nah', to encourage Clementine, but it isn't working – the goat is refusing to stay still as she kicks and runs around the yard.

Grandma is wearing a headscarf and black leather boots, now caked in mud and straw. She is looking despondent and has to go very close to the deaf man's face so he can read her lips.

Apparently the goatherd lives on stale bread but grandma says she's seen him feed fresh bread rolls to the fish in the creek. The walls of his house have large cracks from where moisture has entered and frozen, year after year. He used to have an older woman from the neighbouring village living with him; she was sick and he was looking after her. Then she died and he couldn't afford to pay for gas.

After ten minutes or so – the yard now completely

dark – we give up. Grandma hands the man a folded twenty-crown note for his time. In a loud voice he tells her to take the goat to the neighbouring village where there's another male goat; as he talks his eyebrows appear wild and erratic. He shrugs his shoulders and closes the gate. Grandma drags the uncooperative goat down the dark road, the headlights of passing cars exposing her worried face.

When we get home grandpa is sitting at the kitchen table with the retractable light pulled down. He's sewing a torn glove; the needle, held between a smashed thumb and forefinger, threads its way through his gloved hand. When grandma delivers the news grandpa continues sewing. He asks a few questions, then embarks on one of his meandering tales. The story begins with another man who has a male goat, then meets up with the wife of a distant relative and eventually climaxes around a man nobody seems to know.

He doesn't take his eyes off the glove, inspecting it through his thick, brown-rimmed spectacles, their frame broken and taped together. In front of him, in his white enamel mug with a yellow flower on it, is brown sludge – the remnants of the coffee grandma made before heading out with the goat.

Frozenness

Through the patterned lace curtain and crystalline layer of ice on the window I see smoke rising from a chimney. The smoke is coming out quickly, traveling sideways. The fire is inside the small pink bar that sits at the base of a steep hill. It faces our bedroom window in Lenka's grandparents' house.

Since my last visit the bar has started selling ice-cream. There's a hand-painted sign in the upper left corner, of an ice-cream with red, white and brown scoops sitting in a slightly lighter brown cone. Underneath it, in bold black text on a white background, is the word ZMRZLINA. Translated directly, this means FROZENNESS.

The green tractor is parked outside the bar again. Its trailer, an open cone with the bottom cut off, dominates my view through the relenting ice. I see a dirty ginger cat run past the bar; it pauses in front of a tractor tyre, then exits the window-frame. Soon the tractor will chug off, after the driver's re-fuelling – in the same direction as the cat and the smoke.

The ice on the window is melting; the hill and the

bar – the ice-cream – come into focus through the stripes left by rivulets of water. Below the window, on a wooden chair, is a collection of buttons I will paint: big and small, of many colours, some with threads still attached.

Spring

Grandpa and I cut fence posts on the old circular saw. Some logs are gnarled like his fingers; others white and neat like mine. He's in camouflage, the full outfit. The woodchips hit my neck. I consider the smell of the wood: like biscuits, then vomit, then hospital.

We are repairing the fence broken by intruders. Grandpa tells me to fetch the scythe before struggling through the last hole in the fence to cut grass for his goats in the neighbour's garden. I sit beneath a blossoming cherry tree, and watch his back-straight body through gaps in the fence. Then he calls me over to hold the post while he hammers some of the nails he was straightening yesterday.

After lunch a man grandpa describes as 'The laziest guy alive' will ring our doorbell and beg for milk.

Štefans

Štefan, son of Štefan, is here to kill a goat. Štefan I has taken the other goats to graze on an abandoned plot of land up on the hill. He is very fond of his goats, which all have names: Svetlana, Clementine, Clement I, Clement II. Štefan II will only kill Clement II after several shots of vodka.

Grandma prepares buckets of warm water while her son places a tea-towel over his left shoulder and sharpens his knives. On his way to the goathouse he sits on a ledge smoking; he tells us that he had to shoot Ivan II's crazed dog the other day, that the killing isn't so easy anymore.

It is raining, the goat is dead. Štefan II is in the kitchen, drinking vodka and eating freshly cut goat liver. Soon his father will return from the hill with the other goats. He'll be less comical tonight, won't watch television. More likely he'll read the newspaper in the kitchen, to himself, rather than to whoever happens to be around.

It is still raining. Štefan II can be heard telling a story; it's usually something he's heard on the radio.

His niece, Lenka, sits on a low stool, a relic from her childhood; she's peeling potatoes, their skins dropping into a plastic bowl on the ground between her slippers. Grandma stands nearby, refilling the shot glass, offering more liver. She is listening to her son.

Lines

On the page in my lap I follow the lines on grandpa's face with a stick of willow charcoal. He's sitting at the table sucking bone and cartilage, the left-over meat from yesterday's soup. While I measure his forehead he looks up and finds me staring. 'Dobre?' – ok – he asks. 'Dobre', I reply, hoping he'll continue eating.

I'm being watched by Linda, the sharp, spotty dog, from the daybed beyond grandpa's right shoulder. She sits before a farmhouse and volcano, the distant land described by a tapestry that hangs next to the daybed to hold back the chill of the stone wall.

I shift my gaze to her, measuring her limbs and body size against grandpa's head and the roof of the farmhouse. I follow the bend of the knee and leg then travel over the ridge of the back. I dip into the gully of neck, climb the jaw then cross over the cheek. The dog wants to know if she should come towards me; she's waiting for even the smallest signal. I sit as still as I can.

The line focuses and comes to rest around those expectant eyes. In the dark orbs I catch sight of a tiny window, a glimmer of outside; the windows and eyes are slowly blinking. No longer interested in my inscrutability they come to rest on a front paw, eyelid blinds shutting.

I quietly turn my page and begin my next journey, this time from the damp and drowsy nose.

Pride

On our way to the hay house grandpa is explaining, with his body, how his younger siblings died. Later that evening I'll learn that his younger brother died of lung cancer, his younger sister of a brain injury. This was caused by an accident she had while riding her bicycle to the cabbage fields. As she rode down a steep slope she was startled by a group of children, which sent her toppling over the handle-bars. She died a few years later, after living with headaches.

As I stuff hay into sacks I see a dog across the valley, standing on a kennel, two legs on either side of the pitched roof. With a chorus of other dogs it barks at the empty slopes. I fill twelve bags.

On our way home from the hay house, as I drag the cart full of stuffed sacks over the bridge, grandpa points to the house near the bus-stop where one of his older sisters lives. It's the woman I've noticed peering at me through lace curtains, on the few occasions I've waited for a bus. Another sister, who lives about the same distance from our house, only down the creek, has crooked legs and a large crack in her front window. Last year when we met her on our walk she said that Lenka was looking 'nice and fat'.

Grandpa hasn't spoken to his sisters for many years, despite them all living so close to each other. When I ask grandma why, she simply says 'pride'.

House with three rooms

On an afternoon walk we find a man lying drunk in a field near the river. It's freezing and dark – the man's small body is barely discernible in the long grass. Like the many men who have frozen to death in this field, he would have fallen on his way home from the bar.

As we help the man to his feet he starts crying, his eyes darting and lost. Trembling and holding onto my arm he tells us again and again that his legs are bad, that he is going blind, that since his wife died he lives alone in a house with three rooms.

Bread

Grandma is in the kitchen preparing lunch; she's sitting on a low stool staring through the oven window at the meat. Soon she'll go to her bedroom and get dressed for church. On the radio there's a church service; from the tone of the priest's voice I sense that he might be talking about an event in his life. In the background, among audience members in the church, are the noises I'm listening to: a child asking a question, the clearing of throats and noses, a sneeze, shifting bodies in pews, rustling paper, a row of coughs setting each other off like dominos, a unified murmur in response to the priest finishing his sermon.

Through a light crackle of radio, there is music again: loud voices and tinier ones, an organ muddling through a few wrong notes. The music finishes, everyone sits down, their bottoms settling onto creaky timber. The child persists with a question that goes unanswered.

The sound of the pews takes me back to the church of my childhood. I recall the temptation, when kneeling to pray, to scratch varnish off the pew in front of me. I'd draw lines and the honey-coloured coating would gather under my nails.

The radio sits on an armoire, above shot glasses and knick-knacks. A metre and a half below it is Linda, curled up on the daybed. The blanket she is lying on is covered in hair, small bits of bread and bone. When the priest starts talking I watch as her eyes give up, and remember the boredom.

Directly above Linda, a metre and a half left of the radio, is a clock with a wooden cross attached to it; I'll hear its soft ticking after lunch, when everyone has gone to rest.

The priest is talking. Linda will keep dozing until grandpa and grandma come in from the bedroom, dressed for church. On the stove is a pot of boiling broth, steaming and hissing; beside it, a kettle with water for my tea is on the verge of squealing. The smells of root vegetables, boiling and baking meat, and chopped parsley carry their own air of solemnity.

I pour my tea as grandpa enters through the door

behind me. I can hear him unwrapping one of his aniseed lollies – the bright blue plastic wrappers that map his routines with the goats in the surrounding landscape. He keeps a stash of the lollies in his black leather church bag. Sometimes he asks the nearest person in the kitchen to unwrap one for him. This is when he's already wearing his leather gloves, the shiny black lolly being placed into the black leather palm.

I squeeze my teabag and drop it into the compost bucket behind the armoire. Resting my tailbone against the kitchen bench, I wait for grandma to enter; as the only non-churchgoer, I tend to gravitate towards edges on Sunday mornings.

Grandma sits on the daybed and polishes her shoes while Linda, having rearranged herself into a sphinx, looks on with her tongue out. Grandma always looks rounder on Sundays, in her tighter, monochromatic clothes. Before and after the mass there's a proud, official edge to her and grandpa.

On the radio the people are standing again. A line is forming. They'll each receive their delicate wafer from the priest, then walk up the aisle as it dissolves on their tongue. Later, when the village returns home for Sunday lunch, I'll sit opposite grandpa and wait for my soup.

Ivans

Ivan is in the kitchen following the Easter Monday mass. He's wearing a stained turquoise dinner jacket. His face is red and bloated, vaguely mischievous. It watches attentively as the shot glass is filled by grandma. It bears none of the stiffness of grandpa's Sunday jaw.

Grandma has left the room; he and I, the empty glass, a lone eyelash on his clean white collar.

There's something menacing about Ivan, but today he's warmer. He patted my head when he came in. Soon, when others arrive, he'll be loud and animated, explaining, drinking, explaining – the price of gas, for example.

Later we'll walk up to Ivan II's house. The younger Ivan is all warmth and goodness; I've never felt so welcome in another's house. He has a new daughter, Klara. His son, Ivan III, has orange hair.

Before we leave, Ivan II will offer thirty bags of hay for grandpa's newborn goats.

Good and evil

For the last couple of days I have been spreading compost over the vegetable beds. I shave off thin sections with my shovel then pick out tiny bits of rubbish – bottle tops, soft and hard plastic, rubber, wire, nylon and plastic rope – as well as weeds and roots. One of the reasons for there being so many foreign bits of matter is that grandpa burns all sorts of things and the ashes go on the compost.

It can sometimes take a few seconds to establish whether what I'm looking at is a good or an evil thing. I move my hand through the soil, breaking up the chunks of dark and moist goodness while remaining alert to any miscreants. Each one is picked out and dropped into my prison bucket.

Dirge

I find him straightening bits of wire, which he hooks over the fence. After we'd finished replacing broken palings yesterday, he got angry and his lips were blue. I've been working with him all week, building and repairing the fences. But today he's noticeably unwell; mostly sitting, massaging his hernia, directing me from his rickety wooden chair.

Grandma has been helping us but today she's gone to a sale of nuts and clothes advertised on the public announcement system – a network of loud-speakers on telegraph poles, built during the Socialist era, that deliver messages and play music for the people of the village. At the sale grandma is hoping to find gloves, the ones with dots of rubber on the palms for gripping things.

After lunch a death is announced followed by a long, crackling dirge. Everyone is listening; grandpa holding scribbly wire, neighbours resting elbows on pitchforks, wives pausing in kitchens. They are waiting to hear the name, which they know they will know.

Time

When grandpa cuts grass for the goats, his body hardly moves. His back and legs read eleven thirty while the scythe, or the third hand, turns and cuts with the patience of old age.

After a morning in the garden we slurp our chicken soup. Grandpa comments to grandma that the flies are more aggressive now: whereas they used to simply buzz around, they now fly into his face.

Bananas

Through thick fog we follow the trace of schoolchildren: distant, muffled cries; a torn and muddied drawing; some drops of blood on the few remaining patches of snow, from a nose perhaps. We are led down the skinny dirt path near the river, then over the wobbly footbridge.

From the bridge a man chopping wood comes in and out of focus, his upper body and the glint of his axe blade barely visible through the fog. His house is the first one after the river; it's the point in afternoon walks when one is the furthest from home.

After passing the house with the secret bar, where a woman sells bootleg spirits to widowers and heavy drinkers, we turn right at the road leading to the station then cross back over the river, walk past the old mill and loop back towards the village centre.

Inside the village shop four women attendants stand around the till. They are laughing and talking about Christmas decorations; one woman's tree still hasn't been taken down while another's new tablecloth has already been chosen for next Christmas. We buy bread and milk, some crosswords for grandma, lollies for grandpa.

As we pay, a short, crooked man with a moustache asks the giggling attendants whether there are more bananas, besides the two brown and shrivelled ones in the basket. His words are soft, his eyes mournful. 'No, there aren't', one sternly answers, and another immediately confirms.

Back at home, I rattle the key in the gate lock and wait for the approach of dogs.

Killing day

In the thick fog of early morning the pig hangs from the shed roof with hooks in its ankles. Its hair is being shaved off with long sharp knives. Uncle Štefan, trained as a butcher, rips out the gallbladder and throws it over the fence. A few minutes ago, he fired a bullet into the pig's head and slit its throat, and I watched as the thick, warm blood left its neck and spilled into a large enamel basin. At each point in this process I feel the oldest and tallest of uncle's three sons looking at me, interested in my reactions.

Pig's liver, like red leather, fills plates in the kitchen. Grandma is frying sauerkraut, scrambling eggs with brains. Grandpa can't drink these days; he's sitting in the shed grinding cabbage for his goats, turning the rusted wheel with one hand while the other feeds leaves through the wooden box. Later he'll be kicking one of the goats and complaining to grandma about his drunken son.

Everywhere, meat and organs are being admired, washed, cut, ground, inserted into cleaned intestines for sausages, boiled and eaten. I'm eating my scrambled eggs, rich and creamy from the pig's brain, while the men down shots of slivovica.

It's after midnight; we're in the boiler room where young men listen while the older ones tell fuzzy stories. The air is thick with rendered lard, with shouting and laughter. Uncle makes grandma drink a shot, she says something too loudly then looks down, withdrawing into her lap. She fed the men, now she seems afraid. Today is zabíjačka – killing day.

Pig house

The wheelbarrow, overflowing with shit and straw, gets pushed and steered along the corridor of dirt running through grandpa's sheds, between the garden beds, and finally up a timber plank balanced against the compost heap. I brace myself when approaching the incline, aware that I need enough momentum to get all the way up and still be able to tip out the contents. I then carefully reverse backwards, down the plank, before returning to the pig house for more.

The layers of manure and straw peel off cleanly with the pitchfork; each layer brings the ammonia further up my nose, making my brain itchy.

Grandpa has been sick with a fever, having refused grandma's calls to stay inside and rest. After washing my face and changing my shirt I see him through the glass and lace curtain on the lounge room door; he's sleeping under a purple blanket on the couch, hands interlocked on his chest. Linda is below, asleep on the carpet.

The kitchen is merry that night. We play cards as aunty teases her husband about the way he struggles to hold objects too delicate for his chunky hands. I glimpse a few of his cards, those spilling in my direction. He's a man more gentle than others; his features are soft, his teeth stained. He smiles a lot. Until recently he didn't even drink. Now he drinks whatever aunty gives him but gets very sick.

Grandma comes in to report on grandpa. She sits quietly on the daybed, behind her daughter, who is winning, directing, teasing and filling our glasses. Grandma looks annoyed and worried as she picks bits of bone from around Linda's pillow, shutting them in her palm.

Aunty snaps something over her shoulder; grandma goes to leave, putting a hand on her son-in-law's shoulder, then mine. She embraces both of us, thanking us for our hard work.

Hay

On the hill where grandpa's hay house sits, the hay is being made. I'm not given a scythe, in case I cut my leg. I'm spreading the cut grass with a wooden rake, working near grandma's sister, who smiles and says my rake has more teeth than her. Because she's mostly deaf, like her son Ivan II, she yells. She shows me that it's easier to use the other end of the rake, instead of the teeth, for pulling and spreading cut grass, flattening it out for the sun.

The men are shirtless, cutting in slow sweeping strokes along the slope, sharpening their blades with the stone rattling in their holsters. Every hour or so they stop to drink vodka and smoke; the women keep spreading. An old man I haven't met before – grandpa's 'comrade' – tells stories while younger men listen and laugh.

I work with hunger, thinking about the eggs with wild mushrooms that grandma is preparing, using the mushrooms with spongy bottoms that we picked in the forest yesterday. But when we get home it's soup and baked meat.

Verbs for hay: cut, spread, turn, pile, spread, gather, house.

Broken mirror

I'm cutting my beard when the mirror falls into the bath tub and smashes. Looking down, I see my face all broken, my beard patchy. Suddenly I feel like I'm dreaming. I had started to resent auntie's visiting dog, with its silky hair, those ridiculous flapping ears, the way it interrupted people when they were eating. As I sit on the bath's edge, dreamily staring into the smashed mirror, I hate the dog.

I put on my shirt and go into the kitchen. Lenka is peeling potatoes and I tell her I've broken the mirror. She comes into the bathroom and we carefully pick out the four or five shards in the tub then take them into the kitchen to show grandpa. He looks shocked for a moment then says, 'Nevadí', doesn't matter. The mirror was old and we needed a new one – you won't get a beating, he jokes. He seems pleased with his reassuring role, chewing gristle while patting our concerns down with his greasy hand.

When grandma sees the shards she also says 'nevadí' but is more reserved than grandpa. From the look on her face, as she goes in and out of the pantry, I sense she might be upset about the mirror.

Boots

On my way out to the compost I heard but did not see grandpa. He was perched on a low stool next to the goathouse, scrubbing his boots. As I walk back through the patchwork of sheds, among the hooks, sacks, jars, wire and mice, he doesn't see me, or at least he doesn't turn around.

At the top of the stairs leading to the kitchen door, I turn around and find him looking at me. The look on his face is pensive and curious. When I smile back at him he lets out a huge fart, his gaze returning to his boots.

Potato

After lunch I walk up the Route to Pasture, the road where grandpa takes his goats and where we had once gone to collect willow shoots for grandma's runner beans. In an overgrown plot I find a man I haven't seen before – unshaven, red-faced – feeding three goats with clumps of grass.

I walk past a series of connected houses; they are tiny, broken and sinking into a damp stretch of earth. On my left, a small chained dog startles me from behind a fence; I pick up my pace. The road gets steeper where the bitumen ends. I have to tread carefully along the deep imprints left by tractors in the clay. I smell goats, fermented fruit and shit. Near the top of the hill, beside the stream and willows, there are hissing geese; beside them, an old woman collecting water from the creek.

On my way home I watch a young boy ahead of me. He is kicking a potato; slowly, with little kicks, he tries to keep his game alive.

House blessing

The priest will be here any minute to bless the house. Grandma is nervous about the large pile of wood in the entrance room, about the yard, which seems messy now that its quilt of snow has melted, and perhaps about me coming downstairs while the priest is here. During lunch grandma had cautiously brought up the subject of the wood; she dropped hints while grandpa sucked out bone marrow and picked his way through a bowl of boiled goat meat.

The table in the room directly underneath me, into which the priest will soon enter, is adorned with a special lace tablecloth and a three-tier platter containing exotic and dried fruits, Christmas biscuits and nuts. According to Lenka, it's important that the platter shows as many varieties of biscuit as possible, to impress guests. Grandma and Lenka filled the platter with fresher biscuits and gave the older and softer ones to grandpa, who shared them with the dogs when grandma's back was turned.

The room has been vacuumed, the curtains straightened, the couches perfectly aligned. Every detail of this room has been attended to in preparation for the blessing, while the wood in the entrance room remains piled on grandma's conscience.

A bell is tinkling outside; the priest is nearly here. In a moment or two he'll be led through the front gate by one of his altar boys. This priest has been in the village for about a year, having returned to his homeland from an eight-year posting in Siberia. His predecessor was a controversial figure who used to regularly visit the small pink bar across the creek; his notoriety lives on because of the way he used parish funds to knock down a perfectly good presbytery in order to build what is now referred to by locals as the 'chalet'.

The priest is downstairs. After blessing the house, he leaves with more frankincense, chanting and tinkling bells. Soon he'll be inside the neighbour's house, reciting his blessing and splashing holy water while politely refusing more biscuits.

Shooting star

An early morning walk to the shop, through fog and silence. At the bridge there are workmen on a break; they aren't the destitute locals who wear green and red overalls and are kept busy by the mayor's office, trimming the grass along the creek and so on, but more official workers, dressed in orange high-vis vests. I feel them looking at me with strong, round faces. I try to imagine the taste of beer at this hour.

I return home with my loaf of bread and some offal, blood and barley sausages, a treat only enjoyed by grandpa and me, once made at home, now bought at the shop. Grandma cooks them in the small charred and blackened pan in lard; after a while she splits them open, releasing their contents into the oil until they get crispy. Half-slices of rye bread are used to soak up the fat.

At the front gate there's a Roma man whom I've seen grandpa salute during visits to the hay house. As I get closer, I hear music playing in his pocket. We greet each other; he's probably waiting for grandpa or grandma. His voice is hoarse, his eyes dark and curious. He doesn't know what to make of me, it seems.

I smell alcohol coming from his face, see a star tattoo on his neck. For the briefest moment I taste a life I haven't lived.

Trip to town

The train carriage was empty and had brown vinyl seats. Each seat had been slashed with a single diagonal cut through its middle, each cut stitched up. The thread used to repair the vinyl slashes was a lighter tone of the same brown. Some cuts were more curved, some slightly longer than others.

On the way back from the station we walk along the dark road, past the church and into the gate. There are no dogs to greet us. Inside the kitchen grandpa is sleeping on his daybed, in the darkness. He's made many visits to church these last days, to pray for his recently deceased sister; now he's snoring beside the watchful Linda. Tomorrow's the funeral; in the morning a public announcement and some sad music will remind people.

On the front table there's a plastic bouquet, grandpa's black trilby hat, a brown and white handkerchief with its folds crisply ironed. Before leaving for the funeral grandpa will grind cabbage for the goats.

Candles

From my window I see a man walking out of his front gate holding a bucket; he crosses the road and empties dirty water onto the strip of snow beside the creek.

The woman who, last week, told grandma at church that she wanted to talk to Lenka and me about something, is over there. She's wearing a red parka, hands in pockets. Her scruffy yellow dog is sniffing and running ahead, doing circles with its nose to the ground. Yesterday she caught up with us as we crossed the creek. She asked many questions about Australia then told us about her candle collection. Then she asked whether Lenka's mum might be able to bring her a candle from Australia, when she next comes to visit. We edged away, careful not to slip on the ice – also, would we like to come and see her candle collection one day?

The woman has left the frame. There's a man – no hat, dark clothes – stumbling towards the bar while pulling nothing from his pockets. A dog barks, cars slush by, another dog howls from somewhere above.

Smoke is dribbling from the bar's chimney as the man with no coins looks, then enters.

Radio

Grandpa is paler, thinner, somehow greyer since our last visit. When I come into the kitchen to put water on the stove I find him standing, his back to me, in front of the radio perched above the green armoire. He is slowly turning the dial back and forth as a folk song struggles for voice beneath the loud crackling. I go upstairs to fetch some drawing paper then return to make tea; grandpa is still standing, listening to another semi-tuned song, his fingers now resting on the shelf beneath.

When we arrived in the village last night, and walked through the yard, I was overcome by the smells more than anything: wood smoke, apples – squashed underfoot and lined up in crates – fermenting cabbage and a pot of goat goulash simmering on the stove.

Jumbo

This morning, as I wheel in a cart full of hay, I'm met at the front gate by Linda and her daughter Sydney, named after those who emigrated; both dogs are on heat, their snouts poking under the front fence. I have been collecting the hay alone because grandpa had a 'little' temperature and was confined to boiler room activities.

Štefan II arrives while I empty the bags of hay. He's here to pick up chains for transporting more logs from the mountain. In the kitchen he sits down at the table, eats cake, then goulash, arguing with his father about whether or not Russia has decided to turn the gas back on.

Yesterday he came to cut the long, fat logs in the yard with his chainsaw and we watched with amusement when his dog Jumbo turned up in the yard. Jumbo, pronounced 'Yoomboh' – son of grandpa's now deceased Jumbo – has black fur, dirty whiskers and a chunky body on low legs. When he runs he reminds me of a pig. He had somehow escaped his home, then scratched and bitten his way through one of grandpa's old fences, drawn by Linda's scent. First he got stuck to Linda and then to Sydney on the compost heap.

Uncle is drinking a beer and rolling a cigarette. While being corrected by his son, grandpa presses his knuckles into Sydney's neck; she arches her back in a tortured kind of ecstasy. The conversation shifts to grandpa's ancient red radio, a Polish brand called Euridika. Uncle puts the cigarette in his mouth and closes the door behind him. His tobacco-stained whiskers remind me of Jumbo's.

The radio won't turn on and it is decided that Lenka and I will take it up to Ivan, whose neighbour is good at fixing radios. Grandma is dusting it down, including the plug and cord; her jumper is the same red as the radio. When leaving with the radio in a mesh bag, we tread and dress quietly so as not to wake grandpa. From beneath his heavy arms the dogs watch us, one-eyed, hoping for a chance to escape. Outside the kitchen door Jumbo is begging for more.

Marriage

It's not until mid-morning that I realise that the special turkey lunch we will be having – thirteen of us squeezed into the front room – is to celebrate our recent marriage in Australia, which will finally quell the many questions and hints from extended family members. The mood is less tense than usual: even grandpa, hopelessly anti-social in these situations, is making a special effort to stick around.

Earlier this morning he'd been struggling with all the movement in the house and the lack of attention given to him by grandma. At one point I found him in the kitchen reading the Yellow Pages; every time grandma came in, to get something or check the stove, he'd read out whatever name or company he was looking at. Grandma responded with murmurs, a look of exasperated disbelief on her face.

By the time we are eating poppy seed cake grandpa is again looking uncomfortable; he is pale and stiff-jawed, bolt upright on the edge of a couch a couple of metres from the table where everyone is sitting. His eyes are red; he coughs awkwardly, gripping a walking stick between his legs. After the party he remains there for a few hours, sitting and lying down while watching television.

On my way to bed I catch sight of him through the glazed section of the lounge room door. His good clothes are crumpled; he has his head under the lace curtain – like a bridal veil – as he watches the young men and women gather at the disco across the creek. I can't hear anything because the door is closed but I know he'll be talking to grandma; she is sitting on the armchair beside him, doing a crossword. He'll be telling her what he's seeing, whom he is recognising, while she quietly murmurs her acknowledgements.

Window

Outside the kitchen window: fog, house roofs, barn roofs, tiles, patches of snow, chimneys, dead vines, wire, grandpa's bag, scythes and rakes with wooden teeth hanging against shed wall, sheet of plastic draped over suspended log.

Inside the kitchen window: sleeping and licking dogs, old telephone, loudly ticking Weimar clock, dirty bone-infested rug on daybed, tapestry, newspapers, enamel coffee mug, bread knife, bread crumbs, new tablecloth, geranium branch in glass vase, sugar in glass bowl, teaspoons, creaking radiator, walking stick, shoe-horn, fly swatter, thermometer, light switch, curtain, chair, grandpa's cardigan, jar of milk, hairbrush, postcard from Australia, coats, beer bottle openers, wooden bowl, lolly wrappers, gloves, paperclips, grandpa's logbook, broken pens and pencils, knife with black-taped handle, shadows, tubes of cream, playing cards, furry caps, retractable light, grandpa's cardboard light-shade, light bulb, wire, green cupboard with red knobs, empty sweets tin, gas bill, two radios, broken watches, shot glasses, grandpa's reading glasses, grandpa's sewing basket, pins in red and green pin cushion, scarves, kettle, battery, pills, pegs, matches, sharpening stone, slippers, pile of Catholic newspapers, torch, sticky tape, more wire, dog pillow, string, shoe-shining brush, burnt match, safety pins, scissors, miniature Slovak flag, pliers, keys, more wire, broom.

On the kitchen window: condensation, Linda's paw marks.

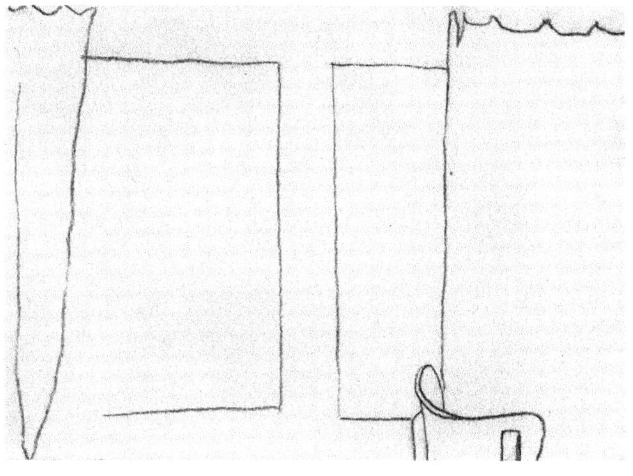

Change

Since our last visit several houses have been painted: the one beside the bar that sells ice-cream, in a bile-yellow; several in a deep, peachy pink; and one in grass-green. The menthol-green house, beside the forest-green bar, still startles me although it has been like this for several visits now.

The special white tablecloth, since I last drew the table, has shifted by a couple of inches, as revealed by the triangular section of cloth now falling over the edge of the table. The table is empty.

Last Christmas there was a multi-tiered biscuit platter and bowl of oranges on the table; last week a vase with plastic flowers briefly appeared; last month a blood-pressure reader occasionally sat there; at various times over the past ten years a shirt might have been draped over one of the chairs.

The scene around the table – doorframe, light switch, picture, tablecloth – remains the same.

Diskoteka

In the early hours of this morning, long after old people had taken themselves to bed, the disco lights were flashing across the wood-panelled interior of the Pelikán, the little bar across the creek.

Pelicans adorn the village crest; they seem to carry two separate meanings among villagers. According to some, pelicans were actually spotted in the village many hundreds of years ago while the more official line points to their Christian significance. Pelicans, once believed to pierce their own breasts in order to feed their young, are a symbol for Christ's sacrifice.

On the pavement outside the bar, groups had gathered in the darkness, banding and disbanding according to the various dramas playing out. There was huddling and embracing, while the very drunken few sat alone on the ledge beside the creek, their heads in their hands. It was only a few degrees above zero but most of the men were in T-shirts and nobody was wearing a hat.

At one point there was a sudden flurry of movement followed by arms and fists flying around.

The instigators were dragged aside, then back to the dance floor, where they flailed around for a few minutes before going in search of more action. The movements of one man, easily recognisable by his striped T-shirt, its white bands glowing in the darkness, made it easy to predict where the next fight would happen.

Six or seven hours later the same groups of fighting and hugging men are walking to church. In neat black and white clothes they walk beside the semi-thawed creek where their cigarettes had been flicked, over the mosaic of green and red chewing gum outside the Pelikán's entrance. They pass the scene of fun and debauchery with their heads down, a few of them glancing across the creek as if trying to recall their roles in a night lost to cheap spirits.

The village is in church for now; a ginger cat stands outside the bar, as if waiting for it to open; it licks itself, then looks down the empty and quiet road.

Great-grandma

Along the winding road to the cemetery we're met by grandma's sister on her bicycle. In her hand are the same yellow flowers Lenka is holding. She's talking loudly, explaining something about not being able to wear her hearing aid because she has a sore throat. Tomorrow she'll go into the forest to pick mushrooms and nettles.

At the cemetery I watch as leaves are swept away, as a snail clings to the side of the slab, as a lone ant navigates and takes a series of panicked turns on the rough cement beside the tomb of Lenka's great-grandparents. Around the graves are plastic petals, burnt matches, a piece of wire still trying to keep some stems together.

I'm remembering her, the woman wearing the headscarf, in the tiny sepia photo beside a round-faced man I never knew, in an oval frame attached to the grave. Three years ago, she was sitting on her bed smiling.

Easter

The wire takes a moment to pierce the outer film of egg; I'm gently pressing the side of the egg with my right index finger so it won't shift in those initial seconds of resistance. Once the wire penetrates, it cuts through smoothly, leaving eight perfectly even, yellow, grey and white cross-sections. I do this to the four or five eggs that grandma has shelled, then lay them out on a plate.

Easter Monday breakfast also includes smoked ham, grated horseradish and finely chopped beetroot. The day before, Lenka took the food in a basket to the early morning mass to get it blessed. None of this food can be thrown out or given to the animals; it needs to be ready for visitors even though we know they won't eat anything. After preparing the table I polish some special-occasion shot glasses while Lenka gathers gifts for the children – miniature koala bears wrapped in plastic, sharks from the aquarium. Only men and boys will come today, to splash the women of the house with water or cologne – the remnant of some pre-Christian custom, according to Lenka.

Grandma is stooped over in the yard, carefully shifting dog poo onto a spade with a stick. She'll be sweeping the path with the yard broom, made of birch twigs, when the first group of men arrive. The husband of Lenka's cousin and his four sons, aged between one and eleven, are ushered into the entrance room; when I come in they are standing in a row, from high to low, like a pan flute.

All the boys, except for the youngest, are carrying canes – plaited willow branches with colourful ribbons attached to their ends. They begin to gently hit Lenka and grandma while chanting their good wishes for the women of the household. The father's tone makes me think that this is a tokenistic procedure in lieu of the water splashing ritual but just when Lenka has let her guard down, the father produces a water bottle. In one swift gesture he has opened the neckline of Lenka's T-shirt and squeezed most of the bottle's contents down her chest. She leans over in shock as he empties the rest of the bottle over her head.

The sons are smiling, the three eldest having taken small bottles of perfume from their jacket pockets, which they now spray Lenka with.

By the end of the ritual the floor is covered in water. Grandma, who has been spared, asks the father to come in for some food; he's declining and indicating that they need to make more visits. A few seconds later the boys are leaving the gate with their mischievous smiles and koala bears. Lenka waves them off in her wet top while grandma mops up, pushing an old towel around the floor with her foot.

Chocolates

As I unload the shopping on the kitchen table grandma notices the chocolates I bought for Lenka's cousin; with a wave of her hand she dismisses them, leaves the room then returns with three boxes, all still in plastic and identical to the one just bought. She points to each of the expiry dates with her finger, grabs a tea-towel, wipes down the oldest box then hands it to me.

Chocolates are mostly given to people on their birthdays and name days. It's quite normal for a box to enter the same house twice, or migrate back to the people who originally purchased it. At any one time grandma's cupboard houses between half a dozen and a dozen boxes. Nobody wants to be left with a box nearing its expiry date because that effectively takes it out of circulation. It also means eating something that people have been conditioned to regard as a form of currency.

The night before I bought the chocolates, Lenka had translated a story we were watching on the news, about a surgeon caught taking a bribe for a heart transplant. The bribe consisted of three thousand euros, two ducks – weighing three and four kilograms – and a box of chocolates.

Business

After handing Jano a folded five-euro note for his day of work grandma disappears inside; a few minutes later she returns with some hotel shampoo sachets, left by us on a previous visit, two-thirds of a large bottle of cola, and an offcut of cloth. Jano is pleased and says he'll make a curtain.

Grandma has been employing Jano, a Romani worker in his fifties, for more than twenty years. The jobs usually involve heavy lifting, wood chopping or emptying the outhouse.

Jano's powerful physique, his even distribution of weight and muscle, and the way he strides up and down a village that is openly hostile to Roma – head down, fists clenched – reminds me of a bull. He has tattooed names scrawled across his forearms and smokes a coarse tobacco that comes in large zip-lock bags.

It is when talking to Jano that I am made acutely aware of the way I stand out here, and how divorced my life is from everyday survival. I feel his eyes closely watching me as he asks, for the hundredth time, how it is I make money. Despite all this he seems to like me – he's told grandma a number of times that I'm a 'dobrý chlop', a good guy.

He only has one word for the West, which includes wealthy countries like Australia. The word is 'business' – pronounced 'bizniss' – and is always accompanied by a gesture of his hand, spiralling downwards as if sneaking its way into a money jar.

This morning I used this gesture for the first time while aunty was telling me about a corrupt mayor. I performed the move self-consciously and without the force and weight of Jano's hand, but it was immediately acknowledged by aunty.

When expressing my shock at the many blatant abuses of power being listed, aunty shrugged her shoulders, unable to understand my surprise. I asked her why the ex-mayor was never arrested, to which she replied, rubbing the tips of her first two fingers and thumb together, that the police and mafia also had their hands in European Union funds.

There are few English words spoken or understood in the village but everybody understands 'business', the word Jano says while turning his open palm round and round like a corkscrew.

Pools

My ears are ringing as grandpa walks off in the direction of the front gate and I lay the wood we have cut into plastic tubs. Through gaps in the fence behind the electric saw I see a man and a woman next door. They are 'town people', in their late sixties; he is bald, darkly tanned, short and solid, a bit like Picasso; she is taller, with broad shoulders, her hair in a bob, like one of Picasso's lovers perhaps. They only come here occasionally, during their holidays.

The man inherited the house a few years ago. Since moving in their possessions, including a microwave oven, television and barbeque, they have been burgled a number of times. Today they are making the most of the sunshine: dressed in their underwear, drinking beer on their freshly trimmed lawn. From their radio I make out a local rendition of John Lennon's 'Imagine'.

Grandpa has wandered over to the bar where he'll be talking to the owner. No longer the notorious drinker he once was, he will probably be eating an ice-cream while telling the story about the medic who stopped to say hello when we were stealing gravel off the side of the road yesterday. Something along the lines of whether there was a cure for old knees, which also means 'old age', followed by laughter. The four buckets of gravel were later spread into the mud in the driveway.

I am sitting on the porch when grandpa returns; after locking the gate he takes out the three or four pieces of junkmail, just dropped in the mailbox. From my elevated position I can see that he is transfixed by a page of swimming pools: chemical blue shapes with little pig-like models that seem utterly alien amid the dusty mid-tones of the yard.

Later that night, while eating his soup, grandpa will tell grandma that he wants a pool, joking that they only cost such and such euros. 'Joj' – gosh – he exclaims, recalling the bright blue shapes.

Other new items I have heard grandpa ask for include an outdoor furniture combo, watches, sausages from Poland and a tractor to drive to church in.

Wealth

Grandpa likes to greet me in the morning, when I enter the kitchen to make my cup of tea, by saying, 'Dobré ráno, malý pánko' – 'good morning, little lord'. By this time, grandpa has fed the goats and is on his second cup of coffee.

Grandpa believes that wealth has nothing to do with money. He likes to say that the truly wealthy man is the one who can decide when he wakes up.

Stories

Grandpa is in the kitchen instead of watching television. He's telling us about his father, about the grenade that had exploded near his head, which had left him with a patch of scalp that moved up and down when he breathed.

Grandpa wasn't yet born when his dad came walking up the village one morning, years after the war had ended; long presumed dead, he looked like a beggar – 'a sack of bones' – in his Russian military coat. Many decades later he would be killed by a falling tree.

I was hearing these stories after a day spent on the mountain with Lenka's uncle and cousins, felling the winter's wood supply. After several shots of vodka, mugs of instant coffee and slices of apple and ricotta cake baked by grandma, I watched as the chainsaw removed a triangular wedge from one side of an enormous beech tree before cutting in from the other. The wedge would make the tree fall in a particular direction but there seemed to be confusion about exactly where this would be.

As the tree started teetering the men dispersed and I watched with horror as it came crashing down in the direction of aunty's husband. He emerged a minute or so later: smiling, his face covered in blood. He had run straight into a 'stromček', a tiny sapling. Over more vodka and cake the incident was mulled over and laughed about. I was urged to keep the details secret from grandpa and grandma.

When grandpa reminisces to Lenka about his father I notice a tear in the corner of his eye. He's telling us that he always wanted stories from his father, like the ones he's telling us, but was told, 'The less you know, the better you sleep'.

Chairs

It's raining, the kitchen is quiet. Grandma is bent over the table doing a crossword from the book we bought at the post office yesterday. She's standing with her back to the door and the passage that runs through to the main part of the house, a position intended to hide her idle pursuits. When the kettle boils she'll make grandpa coffee then take it to the bedroom with a plate of bread and thickly spread lard. Lately, grandpa has been staying in bed until nine or ten o'clock; when he works it's only for an hour or two.

I'm sitting opposite grandma, in grandpa's chair, drinking tea from my favourite tea cup – the small white one showing a cartoon illustration of a blue boy wearing a hat made of newspapers. The first time I sat here was to draw the room from a different angle; it felt like mutiny. Now grandma seems pleased when she sees me sitting in this chair and occasionally resting on the daybed. Many hints have been made to Lenka this trip, mainly from grandpa, about us moving in and taking over the house.

Water

The small church sits within a ring of chestnut trees, on a mountain where we go to get water from the spring and to forage for mushrooms. Each year, on Saint Anna's Day, people from Lenka's village and three others walk up and congregate at the church.

This morning it's hotter up on the hill than we expected. Aunty is telling us to be careful of the horseflies. While the others pick wild sorrel in the meadow, I take bags of plastic bottles down to the stream in the gully behind the church. I put my hands under the cold water coming from a pipe beneath a grotto in which a picture of Saint Anna hangs, splash my face, then fill the twenty or so bottles.

Beside the car, beneath one of the chestnut trees, we look at a small memorial and aunty reminds us about the events of last year's Saint Anna's Day. The church was full, with hundreds of people huddled around its entrance, when a huge storm struck. Everyone stood in terror as the priest commanded them to stay for the duration of the service.

Aunty describes the scene of panic and smoke. As water roared down from the heavens and lightning struck the church and trees, people young and old were being knocked to the ground and 'walking all over each other'.

Where the woman died, under this tree, there now lies a small marble slab, a cross, some flowers and unlit candles. Beyond the fields at the base of the mountain, I see her village and her apricot-coloured house. I calculate the gap between the years engraved on the shiny metal cross to be thirty-nine. I try to imagine the narrowing distance between the crack of the thunder and lightning flashes, the fear of being struck measured against the judgement of the priest and her fellow worshipers.

The wooden heart with a carved crack down its centre, nailed high up on the tree trunk, only becomes visible after a few minutes. Apparently the sculpture was made by the brother of the priest, who had been stood down. Aunty says the brother is 'a cultured man and writer'.

Fishies

In the bar across the creek I drop in for a beer with my mother-in-law and Lenka's aunty. It is clear that the barman – damp brow, no chin, body full of anger – fancies both sisters. Four wives have already left him, he is telling them, but he's never had to move.

An old drinker enters the courtyard declaring, 'All the fishies have died'. People only half listen before returning to their conversation. He leaves distraught, in search of somebody else to tell. The barman is talking about a concoction of honey and daffodil which helps him sleep since giving up smoking. Aunty shows interest so he writes down the recipe for her.

When we leave the bar, we find people up and down the village, leaning over the railing and looking into the creek. Everyone loved seeing the fish, which had recently reappeared. Now the fish are dead.

Speaker

On the public announcement system the woman from the mayor's office announces Mother's Day celebrations at the House of Culture, then the prices per kilo of vegetables for sale outside the preschool, brought in the red van from Poland. Then she loses her breath and for the first time I hear the amplified sound of saliva being swallowed. Light pop music from another era plays before and after.

Ukraina

My morning of drawing starts in the kitchen – dogs, daybed, pillows, cups, teaspoons, table with tablecloth, newspapers, window, curtains, coats, shoes – then moves out to the yard – wooden beams, brooms, washing line, rags, bicycle, pipes, rakes, buckets, stash of wire.

Grandpa is in the shed, hammering something, while grandma and Lenka lay down poison in the attic for the rat we've been hearing each night since our arrival. I'm sitting on the veranda when the doorbell rings – one ring, pause, then two rings in quick succession. Knowing that grandpa won't answer, even if he's heard the bell, I go out and find a woman, possibly in her seventies, with a trolley full of plastic bags and clothes.

She talks too quickly for me to understand but I hear the word 'Ukraina' and remember other people from across the border who have begged for clothes here. Knowing that grandpa won't be any help I say no thank you and yell at the dogs to stop barking. Maybe she could come back later, I say, calling the dogs inside and closing the gate.

I return to my chair on the veranda; the sun has disappeared behind a cloud and it's suddenly cold. I feel the deep topography of her face, its honey-coloured and shiny surface capped by a green velvet beret; her silver teeth. What I feel most is the way her eyes, so loaded with life, had looked into mine.

I place my charcoal pencil on the page and start drawing, tracing the pitch of the neighbour's shed roof, crossing over to our shed roof, then coming down the downpipe bearing grandpa's signature of wire.

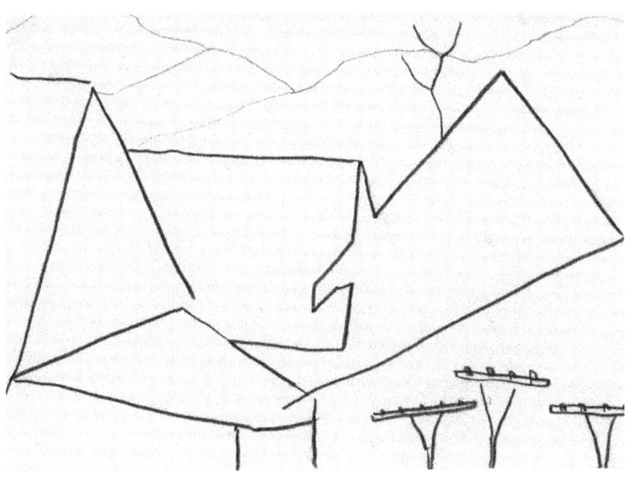

Small breaths

Before becoming ill yesterday grandpa was measuring and cutting logs with a hand-saw, to replace the fences breached by dogs on the scent of Linda's heat. Now he is sleeping in the room directly below, pale-faced and short-breathed beneath a purple blanket. In the armchair beside him grandma stalks her crosswords.

Framed by my window is a view of snowy hills; the furthest are blue, their edges softer without the detail of treetops. Dotted around the village being held by these hills, are houses and startled tree branches. Some houses are neat like grandma's slices of cake, others sagging, cracked or roofless, their fences collapsing into uncut grass. Even the more functional houses aren't completely symmetrical, their lines not quite straight, as if they were drawn without a ruler.

Some houses are proud, others more inward and retreating. These are asking to be left alone, the smoke from their chimneys like the small breaths of grandpa's sickly sleep.

Landslides

The neighbouring village has a new mayor. He's what locals refer to as 'cigan', part of the Romani community and shanty town that occupies a hill opposite the train station. He only finished six grades, and he can barely read, Ivan II is telling me.

After we leave Ivan's, and walk home along the creek, Lenka fills me in on how the new mayor came to power. Apparently the village proper had split their vote between four candidates; meanwhile the cigan guy – cashed up after working in the West – had paid five euros to those in the shanty town willing to vote for him.

The new mayor won with an overwhelming majority. He now lives in a semi-fluorescent orange mansion on one side of the train station, while, according to Ivan II, his voters – living in tiny makeshift homes dotted around the steep valley opposite – face the risk of a potentially disastrous landslide.

Sweet tooth

It's New Year's Eve. Grandpa, grandma, Lenka, the dogs and I are sitting in the lounge watching television. There are news items about New Year's Eve events around the country and warnings about the dangers of fireworks. Then there are two brief stories, one about a kneeling man run over by three cars and another titled 'Hen lays bizarre egg', showing an old and toothless peasant proudly holding her oversized museum piece up to the camera.

During the weather forecast, which predicts the possibility of overnight snow in our region, I notice from the corner of my eye that grandpa is holding his jaw and leaning forward in a strange manner.

We go to the kitchen to get some snacks then return to find grandpa holding a rotten tooth in his palm, which grandma is closely inspecting. When showing us the tooth he drops it, prompting a search under the couch. We find it under Lenka's armchair; while I lift the chair grandpa leans down and picks it up, quickly closing his hand over it and returning his gaze to the television. Grandpa seems unconcerned about the tooth but later mentions that there is a sharp piece remaining, which he says he could cover with some bubblegum.

After the news there's a retro variety show, for old people who stay at home on New Year's Eve, followed by a second one. Before eleven pm I go up to bed, unable to get through the hour or so leading up to the fireworks.

I'm woken at midnight by a series of explosions, some from the bar across the creek. Lenka comes up and tells me that the dogs are terrified and hiding under the couch; I can hear grandpa trying to reassure them – they aren't guns, it's only kids with fireworks, he tells them. For the next twenty minutes I lie listening to the crackling, banging and whistling noises, watching streaks of green and yellow lights flash by. Then I fall back to sleep.

Feet

I eat my breakfast then go out into the freezing cold yard; I trim my toenails then dig into their corners, for the first time using the hook-like blade on the toenail clippers. I return inside and put my feet in the bath and thoroughly soap, scrub and rinse them.

Last night we watched a documentary about a well-known Slovakian priest who shelters homeless people in this region. As I clean between my toes I remember a scene in which one of the homeless men had washed his feet in a public toilet in a train station. The man had been in and out of the priest's shelter according to whether or not he was on the drink, alcohol being strictly prohibited; at the moment of washing his feet he had been back on the streets for a few weeks.

When seeing the man wash his feet, a bit awkwardly because he had to do it in a basin, I had felt a bit ashamed. Here I was, in a warm home with excellent washing facilities, and I never even considered my feet.

Photo

The small sculptures were housed in custom-built display boxes with dusty Perspex covers. Rather than hanging on his cross, Christ was small and often lying in contorted agony. The sculptures were in various states of disrepair, some bruised and with chunks missing, which added to the pain they held.

In the museum there was mould on the walls; pot plants and fire extinguishers sat around the floor. The atmosphere of humility and neglect was absolutely right for these works; the decaying spa town, where people go to drink and bathe in healing mineral waters, and the lovingly created though odd vitrines seemed to complete the sculptures.

In the evening, after returning from our journey to the mountain town, grandma, Lenka, the dogs and I watch television, while grandpa sleeps in the neighbouring bedroom. Beside a plate of peanut shells on the coffee table is a photo of grandma and grandpa. I pick it up and look at it more closely, at their furry caps and jackets, at grandma's black leather boots – possibly the same pair she now wears in the garden. I look at the way her hands are clasped together, the way his right hand holds her left elbow. Grandpa's face is the same only stronger, his features more severe, while grandma's face is thin and fraught. Underneath the photo, in medieval font, is the name of the place of healing.

Off/on

By ten thirty this morning it was thirty-eight degrees. People were hiding indoors, at home or in the bar. I was in the lounge room noticing the way the heat made each and every detail seem significant: the way people walked, a straw hat, some orange shoelaces, the unfamiliar sight in the village of a trimmed beard.

By mid-afternoon there was the slightest of breezes; I watched the gently breathing curtain reflected in the television screen. It was daytime; the curtains were open; the television was off.

It is night-time; the curtains are drawn; the television is on. Grandma is about to watch a show.

Patrik

The last time grandpa and I went to the hay house we made a bonfire; from either side of the fire we watched the flames dance upwards, their orange sparks taken by the wind. We'd spent a couple of hours stuffing hay into sacks, tossing them down the slope – freeing them from branches using the wooden-toothed rake when they got snagged.

The cart with twelve or so sacks was parked by the gate while we stood among nettles and squashed apples, grandpa crunching dried leaves in his hand as he nodded in agreement with the flames. For once we weren't there to carry out grandpa's work ambitions but simply to be together; we were taking stock of something.

The hay house was accessed by a steep track that ran up the back of an abandoned property; the small plot of land and half-built concrete carcass sit between the Little Cart Path, a grassy laneway that leads to the Route to Pasture, and the surrounding fields. Grandpa had justified building on public land by pointing out that before the Russians arrived, and confiscated the land, it had been owned by his family.

While lying on his deathbed grandpa saw the smoke rising above the hill and immediately knew that his hay house was burning. It turned out that a young man called Patrik, the son of a now-deceased village sex worker, had been taking shelter from his violent stepfather, when he accidentally set the hay and timber structure alight with a cigarette.

I knew who Patrik was. Our name isn't common here. I'd also heard aunty say that he was a distant relation after he came begging for money at our gate. And yet it's only when grandma tells us this story that I realise he would have been the person I'd seen fifteen years ago, after I first ventured up the Route to Pasture. He had been a few metres ahead of me, his steps erratic and hard to decipher. It had only been when passing him that I understood what he was doing. He was kicking a potato.

Ants

Grandpa had a red A4 logbook in which he recorded the weather, gas usage and noteworthy events such as the birth of animals. He did this at the kitchen table, usually while drinking his morning or evening coffee. He used a pencil, which he sharpened with a paring knife, and a ruler.

I write in tiny notebooks and sometimes on postcards; each day I record my observations and the stories told to me by Lenka, using a fine felt-tipped pen. When grandma sees my writing she says it looks like 'mravce', or ants.

God

As we walk back from the skip with our hay carts, where we had taken some of grandpa's junk, I realise how blistering the heat is. I notice the Sahara sand they've been mentioning on weather reports: small clouds of dust travelling down the road a few metres at a time as if trying to get through the alien territory unnoticed.

Jano wipes his face with his T-shirt and I see his belly. He points out each newly blossoming tree – apple, pear, plum. I think he's telling me that he was lying in bed last night wishing God would take him, that he wants to go and live with the priest who helps the homeless and sick in this region.

A couple of doors up from grandma's house he tells a woman crouched in a flower bed 'God bless your work', to which she responds 'May God hear you'.

Goose

Sunday morning: a goose has escaped. It wasn't eating well and its new lightness meant it was able to fly over two fences. I'm sent along to help aunty's boyfriend, the only other non-church-goer, to recapture it while another goose lies snug in the oven.

I'm excited – the opportunity to see another garden compound is rare.

Wine

While cutting through knee-high grass and nettles, using aunty's new whipper-snipper, I notice the goatherd scything through a section of land in the abandoned property next door. His wiry frame hardly moves as the blade casually wipes away six months of undergrowth.

Every few minutes he removes the smooth sharpening rock from its holder, about the size and shape of a sardine, to sharpen the ancient-looking metal, in swift alternating strokes. It rests in a metal pouch clipped to his back pocket, in a small pool of water. Together they make a soft clanking noise that reminds me of a distant cowbell.

I've been getting to know him this visit. Sometimes he lets himself into our garden through a broken section of fence. He brings gifts: bags of pears, greengages and walnuts. In broken dialect we usually talk for a few minutes, about his goats mainly. I have to speak loudly because he's deaf; he never says goodbye when leaving.

When he sees me working, particularly with a

scythe, he always tells me to slow down and take a rest: 'pomaly … oddýchni'. This is something grandma also says and I've realised it's to do with the manner more than the fact of my working.

I take off my protective mask and earmuffs and go over to say hello. I'm soaked with the juice of fallen apples, which the plastic cord of my machine has been whipping through. As I approach the goatherd he is scolding the goats for eating apples; apparently it gives them diarrhoea, a fact that Ivan II, a fellow goat farmer, finds hard to understand. I ask if his goats have names; he only tells me the name of the one still eating an apple: Julia.

The goats respond to their owner's grunts by moving away from the branches before shifting over to other apple trees. Their eyes look sideways, almost backwards; they are stubborn, like their leg muscles, and cheeky.

We express our greetings then fall into silence. When he sees the goats chomping at the ends of low-hanging apple branches again he picks apples off the ground and starts pelting them at the goats. They run off and he follows, disappearing into a paddock of nettles and mint leading down to the stream.

A bit later, when I'm almost finished with the cutting, he shows up again holding a bunch of purple grapes. When I express my pleasure in them he says something then disappears, giving me the impression that I should follow. A few minutes later I end up in his yard, surrounded by a series of animal and human habitations and a fence covered in grapes. In the yard are some old bus seats, their upholstery in tatters, some sticks leaning against the wall and half a dozen kittens, lounging and hiding around the chairs.

The goatherd explains to me that he used to make wine but doesn't drink anymore.

Linda

I spot Linda bolting into a field of overgrown grass before disappearing behind a crumbling barn. I'm piling broken concrete into wire cages, on the sloped section of garden where aunty hopes to create a level space for a gazebo.

Both the neighbouring property and the one beyond, where Linda went, are abandoned; now that the fences have fallen, and grandpa isn't here to fix them, the three gardens are one.

Grandma comes outside and I tell her that Linda has escaped. She listens to my broken message with a furrowed brow then dismisses my concern, her hand slapping the air, 'Nevadí', it doesn't matter.

Linda was brought into the kitchen by Lenka's aunt during one of our visits many years ago. She was found by the side of the road, shivering in the winter rain a hundred or so metres from the Romani shanty town. It was assumed by everyone that night that she'd escaped the knife and goulash pot. Since moving in she has twice been run over and lost countless offspring, most recently her daughter and companion Sydney. Most of the pups were dumped in the creek by grandma; the odd one went to a family.

Since grandpa passed I've noticed that grandma's mood toward the dog has softened. Whereas she used to yell at Linda and sometimes hit her – angry at grandpa for giving her good meat – the two of them have become largely inseparable. In the morning, when the sun streams in through the windows in the front room, grandma knits and Linda lies curled up at her feet; during the afternoons they're in the garden, Linda nosing around while grandma pulls weeds and waters the vegetable beds.

Linda will return in a few hours. She'll be waiting outside the front gate, her tail wagging, when we head out for an evening walk; she'll brush past my legs and run into the yard, her uncut nails tapping along the tiled porch as she heads back to the kitchen.

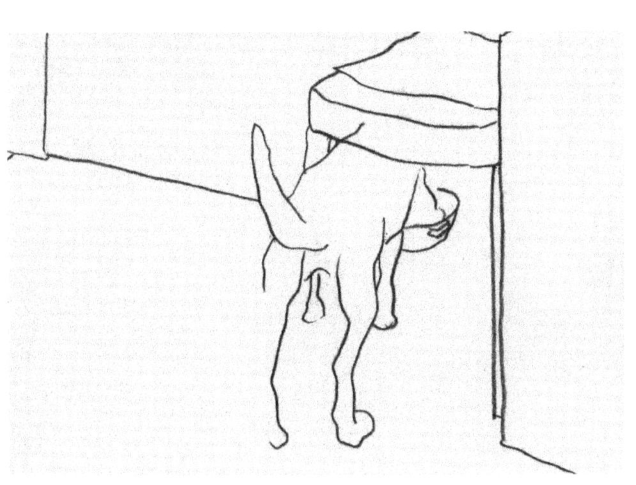

The peasants

I see the goatherd first, then watch as a procession of villagers go by, each pulling a cart packed with junkmail leaflets. I remember the public announcement made yesterday, about the truck coming to exchange junkmail for toilet paper.

When grandpa was alive grandma had to hide any advertising, particularly in summer, when he would go on and on about how beautiful everything looked. She hid any new junkmail among the piles of older leaflets in the basement; they sit there still, beside the furnace, because their glossy paper is no good for burning.

A little while later I see aunty leaving through the front gate; she has packed grandpa's old hay cart with paper – pages and pages of mass-produced meat, televisions and gardening equipment. We'll celebrate with vodka and klobasa – sausages cooked over the fire – after she returns with seventeen rolls of toilet paper.

Songs

We drink slivovica with aunty as she tells us stories about the family – how Lenka had gone to Australia, how we had come to meet. I didn't know much about Pavol, Lenka's great, great-grandfather. He was the one who initially went to Australia with his wife and two younger children in the 1930s, returning twenty or thirty years later, having been deported for being a communist. On his return to the village he moved back into the family home, tended by his eldest daughter who had been married off at sixteen. He communicated with his other children, who had remained in Australia, through the post.

Aunty makes a gesture of a rim circling around her head, remembering his fancy hats. By that time his wife had died and he'd taken to the drink. Most mornings he'd tell his daughter that he was going to the post office before zig-zagging home a few hours later.

There's a story about Pavol sealing an envelope with what he thought was a roll of sticky-tape sent by his son. One day he complained to someone that the tape didn't stick well when sealing his envelopes, so he was having to add glue to it. Eventually it was pointed out to him, by his son receiving the letters, that it was audio tape. A remnant was salvaged and played and a group of them listened to his children singing traditional Slovak songs.

I'm a little drunk as we speculate that I too might be returning home: the Celts were in this region long before any Slavs turned up. It's late as Lenka and I sit with our heads out the window breathing in the cool night air; the creek is flowing more loudly than usual, following the afternoon storm. A big moon shines overhead, its light painting the village silver.

Gazebo Books
PO Box 375
Summer Hill
New South Wales 2130
Australia
gazebobooks.com.au

First published 2021

National Library of Australia
Cataloguing-in-Publication Entry
Hartigan, Patrick, 1977-

First edition
ISBN 978 0 6451030 4 5

Cover and interior design by Mountains Brown Press

www.ingramcontent.com/pod-product-compliance
Lightning Source LLC
LaVergne TN
LVHW052354100826
845147LV00013B/835

* 9 7 8 0 6 4 5 1 0 3 0 4 5 *